GEORGE ANCONA

DANCING IS

E. P. Dutton   New York

to Barbara Brenner

The marzipan portrait of George Ancona
on the facing page is by Trini McClintoc.

Library of Congress Cataloging in Publication Data

Ancona, George.   Dancing is.

Summary: The author briefly explains some dances of
various countries around the world.
1. Dancing—Juvenile literature.
2. Folk dancing—Juvenile literature.
[1. Folk dancing. 2. Dancing] I. Title.
GV1596.5.A52 1981 793.3 81-3296
ISBN 0-525-28490-7   AACR2

Published in the United States by Elsevier-Dutton
Publishing Co., Inc., 2 Park Avenue, New York, N.Y. 10016

Published simultaneously in Canada by Clarke,
Irwin & Company Limited, Toronto and Vancouver

Editor: Ann Troy

Printed in the U.S.A. First Edition
10 9 8 7 6 5 4 3 2 1

WHAT DANCING IS TO ME

When I was a little boy, my father taught me to dance. He would come home from work and put on a record. The music was from Mexico, the country where he grew up. He showed me how the cowboys there would dance the heel-stamping *zapateado*. I would imagine their boots raising the dust on a platform set outside the bunkhouse while guitars played and the men sang.

Today it is my turn to dance around the living room with my children. When I dance, I share my feelings with others. With this book I hope to share my feelings with you.

Dancing is
a skip

and a hop

and a kick

and a stomp

and a run

and a jump

and a wiggle

and just feeling good.

Dancing is
moving to music.

To dance,
just listen to the music.
The rhythm will tell you
how to move.

10

SPANISH FLAMENCO DANCE

People dance alone

GREEK SAILORS' DANCE

or together.

CONTRA DANCE

There are dances for three people,

and dances for four people,

and dances for lots of people.

ISRAELI *HORA CHEFFER*

People dance
to celebrate.

There are dances
for special days
of the year,

and dances
for the new seasons,

ENGLISH MORRIS DANCE

23

and dances
for special events.

There
are
dances
that tell
stories.

Once upon a time, a frog

danced

in a pond

with the fish, the crab and the turtle.

The frog dove to the bottom of the pond

and became the beautiful Princess Mandodari.

The princess
was covered
with jewels.

Her eyes
were like those
of the deer.

Ravana, the ten-headed king, who was powerful

Rising from the
pond, she moved
like the swan.

and arrogant,

saw Mandodari
and fell in love
with her.

He took her
to the Island
of Lanka,

where
she became
his queen.

All over the world
people have their own dances.
When they move away,
they teach their children
the dances of the old country.

RUSSIAN SPRING DANCE

By dancing, people remember
the lands they came from.

THE UKRAINE

ITALY

THE PHILIPPINES

SWEDEN

IRELAND

THE DOMINICAN REPUBLIC

HUNGARY

NIGERIA

GUADELOUPE

MEXICO

CHINA

Some of these
dances are performed
mostly by men.

BRAZILIAN *CAPOEIRA*

Others are performed
mostly by women.

Many of the old dances changed
and became new dances.

ENGLISH CLOG DANCING
mixed with
African steps
and other dance forms
to become
AMERICAN TAP DANCING.

Dances change
from place to place
and people to people.

GEORGIA CLOGGING

APPALACHIAN CLOGGING

When some people decide
to make dancing their work,
they go to school.

MODERN DANCE

AFRO-CARIBBEAN DANCE CLASS

They train so that some day they
can dance for other people.

BALLET CLASS

But most
people
dance
because
it's fun,

and to share
happiness and the joy
of being alive.

THE DANCES IN THIS BOOK

people from Nigeria, West Africa. Women dance in honor of their chief and to show their strength and gracefulness.

CHINA, RIBBON DANCE Inspired by sheets of dyed silk drying in the wind, this ancient festival dance dates back almost two thousand years to the Han Dynasty.

MEXICO, *JARANA* The typical dance from the state of Yucatan in southern Mexico. It incorporates modified Spanish footwork with Mayan Indian rhythms.

GUADELOUPE, *BELE* A traditional village dance, festive in nature, usually seen in Guadeloupe, Martinique and Trinidad.

THE DOMINICAN REPUBLIC, *MERENGUE* The typical folk dance from the rural areas of the Dominican Republic. It has grown to influence much of Latin American music or *salsa*, which means "sauce" in Spanish.

HUNGARY, *VERBUNK* OF SZATMAR A dance used to recruit men into the Hungarian army during the eighteenth century.

34 BRAZILIAN *CAPOEIRA* A martial arts dance between men who make aggressive moves and spectacular leaps over each other, but never actually touch. This form of dance was created by African slaves when they were prohibited from fighting. Today it is performed by men, women and children.

35 MIDDLE EASTERN BELLY DANCE The traditional woman's dance of Middle Eastern countries. It may have originated as an aid to childbirth, to entertain the sultans, and for women to entertain each other. The veil is sometimes used as part of the dance.

36 ENGLISH CLOG DANCE A dance performed with wooden-soled shoes that was developed by the miners of northern England. There are two styles of English clog dancing: Northumberland and Lancashire.

37 AMERICAN TAP DANCE In addition to English clog dancing, other dance forms influenced tap dancing. These include: African ritual dance, Irish clogging, Afro-American social dancing, Iroquois and Algonquian Indian dances, English music hall and American vaudeville dance.

38 GEORGIA CLOGGING One of the many variations of clogging performed today at county fairs and exhibitions. In-stead of wooden shoes, leather shoes with large, moving metal taps are worn.

38–39 APPALACHIAN CLOGGING An American descendant of English and Irish clog dancing. It has become the traditional dance of the Appalachian Mountain people. Shown is a precision routine called The Rainbow Stroll.

40 BALLET An art form for the theater in which stylized dancing to music tells a story. It originated in France. To become a ballet dancer, the student must train to move in special ways: body erect, legs turned out and toes pointed. Girls learn to dance on their toes; boys learn to make spectacular leaps.

41 MODERN DANCE The dance form that developed in this century as a protest against the formal movements of classic ballet. Movements are more natural and personal. American dancers made it the art that it is today.

AFRO-CARIBBEAN DANCE These dance forms resulted from the blending of African movements with the Indian and Spanish rhythms of the islands in the West Indies. Compared to European dance, these forms use a freer and more natural body movement.

42 Top row: Swedish *HAMBO*; *VEJIGANTE* MASK DANCE from Puerto Rico; Latin *SALSA*.
Middle row: Policewoman at West Indian Carnival; bride and father doing the WALTZ; CLOGGING class.
Bottom row: *BAVNO ORO*, a Macedonian line dance; *POLKA* from Poland; West Indian *REGGAE* dancing.

43 Top row: The Ukrainian *HUTZULKA*, a peasant dance from the Carpathian Mountains; Jewish folk dance; MORRIS DANCE called Leapfrog or Glorishears, from England; Russian TWO-STEP called *Karapyett*.
Middle row: Bulgarian *BUCIMISH* dance; Israeli couple dance called *Rakefet*; Swedish folk dance; VIRGINIA REEL, which is a traditional contra dance.
Bottom row: A dance from Trinidad; Scottish country dance; Mexican dance from Vera Cruz; American SQUARE DANCE.

44–45 ENGLISH COUNTRY DANCE Called Sellinger's Round.

THANK YOU

For making this book possible by sharing their joy of dancing and knowledge with me, I should like to express my appreciation to:

The children of both Haverstraw Elementary School and the Green Meadow School, as well as their teachers, principals and friends

Trini McClintoc, who helped with the research for the project and the search for the dancers; and Liz Roach, who helped with the making of the prints

Aida, Oriental dancer
Reynaldo Alejandro, The Philippine Dance Company of New York
Dr. Tony Barrand, Squire of Marlboro Morris and Sword
Susan Brody, MAFolkdancers
Marie Brooks, Children's Dance Research Theater
Sandy Connolly, ABC Nursery
Brian Demarcus and Doug Baker, Green Grass Cloggers, Inc.
Dinizulu and his African Dancers, Drummers and Singers
Maria and Carl Fredrickson
Maria Giacone, Dansloric Folk Ballet
Ruth Goodman, Israeli Dance Division, YM and YWHA of 92nd Street, New York City
Chuck Green and LeRoy Myers, The Copasetics
Bertha Hatvary and Beverly Francis, The Country Dance and Song Society

Kazuko Hirabayashi and Mirta Rosello, Dance Department, SUNY at Purchase, New York
Robert Houghton and Enid Kuperman, Hudson Valley Scottish Country Dance Society
Indrani, Classic Indian dancer
Anesti Kamouzas and Michael Maroutsis, H.A.N.A.C. Senior Citizens Center, Astoria, New York
Jeff and Mara Karg
Orest and Andrij Kyzyk, Verkhovynchi Ukrainian Dance Ensemble
Charlene Liu, Young People's Chinese Cultural Center
Mickey Long, Bosilek Bulgarian Dance Ensemble
Loremil Machado, Afro-Brazilian Dance Company
Kalman Magyar, Hungaria Folk Dance Ensemble of New York City
Louis Mofsie, Thunderbird American Indian Dancers
Roy Moyer, UNICEF
Stanley Pelc, Polish American Folk Dance Company
Clemente Pena, Club Dominicano
Tina Ramirez, Verdery Roosevelt and Judy Hogan, Ballet Hispanico of New York
Bonnie Roberts, Buckwheat Cloggers
Poli Rogers, Puerto Rican Dance Theater
Sasha Russian Dance Ensemble, Waldwick, New Jersey
Freddy Sverdlove, The Royal Scottish Country Dance Society
Maria Uyehara, American Museum of Natural History
Bill Vanaver, The Vanaver Caravan
Pat Velderman, Swedish Folk Dancers of New York